CROSS CREEK RANCH

JODI BASYE

Copyright © 2022 by Jodi Basye

All rights reserved.

No part of this book may be reproduced in any form or by any electronic or mechanical means, including information storage and retrieval systems, without written permission from the author, except for the use of brief quotations in a book review.

CHAPTER 1

La Plata County Fair

Rachel Meadows heaved the heavy sack of grain from the truck bed and shifted its weight to center on her shoulder. She eyed the other bag and bunched her lips in contemplation. The walk from the parking lot to the livestock barn was quite a way. Did she want to make two trips in this ninety-degree August heat?

Suck it up, Rach.

Crouching below the tailgate of her '78 Ford Highboy, she shimmied the second bag onto her other shoulder. She made her way through the fairgrounds parking lot, avoiding the crowds of people milling around food trucks outside the exhibit hall. A gaggle of girls hovered outside the entrance of the steer alley, blocking her path. She stopped, cringing at the knots forming in her neck muscles.

Maybe not the best idea to grab both bags at once.

"Excuse me." Rachel shifted the bags higher on her shoulders and forced a smile.

Jessica Stanley looked Rachel over. "Quite the farmhand, aren't we?" She feigned a tone of being impressed, but the smirk tugging at the corner of her lips said otherwise.

Her followers snickered, none of them making eye contact or clearing the way.

"I'm not afraid to get my hands dirty, if that's what you mean." She couldn't help raising an eyebrow as she flashed a glance at Jessica's acrylic fingernails that matched her bright pink tank-top.

"Clearly." Jessica wrinkled her nose. "Come on, girls. Let's go have some fun." She led her posse of pink toward the food trucks, the lot of them giggling and looking back over their shoulders.

Rachel hauled the feed bags the rest of the way to her corner of the barn and dropped them into the dirt. She slumped down to sit on the bags and leaned back against her tack box, wiping the sweat from her forehead with the long sleeve of her t-shirt.

She shouldn't let Jessica and her Cavender's catalog clones get under her skin. Most kids here were just as hard-working as she was and were generally helpful. Still, Rachel was the outsider and kept to herself. Even if part of her wished she had friends or someone to care about, it was best to stay unattached. This year would be her last at the fair, and as soon as she graduated high school, she'd be burning rubber as far from this town as her truck would take her.

She fished out a jug of water from the box and took a long drink. A family walked down the barn's alley, looking at the market steers and taking turns sipping on fresh-squeezed lemonade. It was everything a family should be. The two young children pointed at the different breeds of cattle, and their parents walked behind, hand in hand, reading the animals' names from the signs hung over each stall.

Rachel blinked back the burning sensation behind her lashes and sniffed. She hadn't known that kind of fun family atmosphere since the car accident four years prior. Now it was just her.

She was relieved when Child Protective Services had placed her with a family who had a barn for her animals. Farm life was all she'd ever known, and the prospect of holding on to that one piece of normalcy after her parents' deaths had been her lifeline.

It hadn't been the life she'd hoped for, though. She'd managed to talk her foster parents into letting her continue her 4-H involvement, but every bit of effort had been on her shoulders. To them, she was nothing but a monthly check and someone to do their chores.

She smiled at the little girl in her pink cowgirl boots as the family came closer.

"Do you want to pet him?" Rachel looked at the parents for approval.

"Go ahead, honey." The mom gave the girl a gentle nudge on the back. The small boy ducked behind his dad's legs and peeked around.

"Here, let me turn him around." Rachel tugged the lead-rope's free end and turned around her Black Angus steer, Sully, so the little girl could pet his nose.

Excitement danced in her eyes. "Mommy, I want to be in 4-H when I grow up."

Rachel's heart clenched. She remembered so clearly the enchantment of the fair at that age. The hot funnel cakes, the projects on display, and all the animals to see—it had been her favorite time of year. She couldn't wait to turn eight and be a part of something so magical.

She'd had five years to experience a life where she thrived in 4-H programs, from cake decorating to rabbit breeding to market beef. Five years of working with her parents and learning from their experience, and then it had all been ripped away. Now, it was the only piece of sanity she had left, something she clung to in order to keep her parents close.

Unfortunately, four years after their death, the shine of the trophies dulled, and the bright lights were browning, on the verge of blinking out. Soon she would be eighteen and out on her own. She'd no idea how to go on with it all. How could she move on with building a new life without leaving her parents behind?

The little girl patted Sully on the nose, and the family continued on their way. Sully nudged the back of Rachel's legs. She needed to walk him around before he got too stir-crazy. Besides, she had no one else to enjoy the fair with, but at least she had him. He ambled next to her toward the dirt lot outside the barns. With no one to support her efforts, she'd had to narrow her 4-H projects down to just one steer, bought with the little savings she had from the steer she'd sold last spring.

She never competed with the specially bred market animals most kids here had. He was just an average steer she'd bought from a local farmer, but he was tame and faithful as an old dog.

She led him to a patch of grass over by the old racetrack behind the carnival area. While her buddy tugged and munched the grass, she leaned back, propping her elbows on the white rail fence that lined the old track.

Bright blue Colorado skies stretched from mountain top to mountain top overhead. She shouldn't let herself wallow in self-pity. She lived in a breathtakingly beautiful place, had her dad's old truck and trailer, and because she'd been taken in by the Johnsons, who had a barn and a few acres, had been allowed to keep her horse, Dante. The fact she hadn't lost Dante was nothing shy of miraculous. Closing her eyes against the bright sun, she let the warmth of summer wash over her.

The blaring of a loud bell from a carnival game went off, and Sully, startled by the loud noise, bolted. The jerk of the lead rope yanked her arm, nearly pulling it out of its socket. She grabbed for the end of the rope, but it slid through her grasp, leaving a stinging rope burn in its place.

"Sully!" Rachel ran after the deranged bovine.

Oh, please don't go through the carnival.

What had she been thinking, bringing him over here? He took a sharp turn to the left through a gap in the rails and sprinted around the old racetrack like he was racing for the breeder's cup.

This can't be happening.

People gathered around the track to watch the show, laughing. Rachel ran after him but gave up three-quarters of the way around the track, throwing her hands in the air. Chasing after him was only going to push him farther. She bent forward with her hands on her knees, panting.

Sully stopped a few hundred yards ahead. She slowly worked closer to him, hand outstretched. His eyes widened as she approached, and his head raised. A warning he was about to make a break for it again.

Crouching down, she spoke low and calm to him. "Hey boy, enough of that now, alright?"

He lowered his head and blinked long lashes, sides heaving in the August heat.

"That's it. You ready to go get some water?" Keeping low, she kept her crouched posture and worked her way closer in a duck walk. She reached out a tentative hand to the end of his lead rope and—flash! Rapid clicking and flashing from a photographer behind her spooked the steer, and off he went again.

Sighing, she resisted the urge to pick the photographer

up like a sack of grain and pitch him over the fence. There was no point in running after Sully now. She had to find a way around him instead.

Suddenly, he found another gap in the rails. Bucking and kicking, he darted back toward the livestock barns. A six-foot chain-link fence blocked her way. She scrambled up over it, ripping the sleeve of her shirt, and ran ahead to cut him off from the other side.

Pushing sweat-soaked wisps of hair away from her face, she rounded the horse barns, half running, half walking, and sides aching. Here he came around the other end of the barns and headed straight for the busiest part of the fair, scattering people like geese in a barnyard.

He wasn't going to stop—Lord help her. Sully was headed straight for the food trucks. Panic seized her, and she side-stepped to block his path when a tall figure darted out and deftly snatched the end of the lead rope, pulling the steer to a stop.

Relief washed over her, but a wave of light-headedness quickly replaced it. A pair of warm brown eyes twinkled at her from under a straw Stetson hat. A tingling sensation swept up the back of her neck and into her face. She froze. She needed to say something, anything, but the words stuck in her throat.

"Lost something?" His lips tugged up at the corner with amusement.

"I uh—um, yeah, thanks." Her heart pounded like a trip hammer. *Come on, Rach, you can do better than that.* She shook her head and let out a short laugh. "Really, thank you. That was about to turn into a major disaster."

Her rescuer tipped his hat up with a fingertip and nodded toward the food trucks and exhibits and laughed. "Yeah, that could've been bad."

Taking the lead-rope from him, she folded it in her

sweaty palms and nodded back to the barn. "I'd better take him back and get him watered."

Sully, calm as a kitten now, nudged her hand, smearing slimy, stringy saliva across her palm.

"Thanks again." She forced a sheepish smile and started back, ready to crawl into her tack box and hide for the rest of the weekend.

"Morgan Cross." He thrust a hand out toward her, and she wiped her palm on her jeans before taking his.

"Rachel Meadows." She forced a smile past the heat burning in her face. Her mom would've tanned her hide for being so short with someone who had just helped her. The least she could do was introduce herself.

Why was he still standing there smiling at her? Not that she should mind. He was the best-looking guy she'd seen—ever. She swallowed down the butterflies floating up inside her. She had no business with butterflies. If life had taught her anything, it was that nothing good ever lasted. This was no Cinderella story, and a knight in a shining Stetson was likely to turn into a rat when the clock struck midnight.

CHAPTER 2

Morgan pressed his lips together to smother the smile that rose to the surface. The blooming red flush creeping up Rachel's face told him she wouldn't be likely to share in the humor of this moment. But seeing that steer race around the old racetrack was the most entertaining thing he'd ever seen at the fair.

She pushed back wet strands of tawny hair from her damp forehead and returned a weak smile.

"Thanks again." She turned back to the livestock barn, and her shoulders slumped as she walked away. Something inside him was pulled along with her, like a mule in a pack string.

"Wait up." His long legs only needed two strides to catch up to her. "I don't think I've seen you around before."

Lame.

Of course, he hadn't seen her around. Though he spent some time here in Durango, his family's ranch was closer to Pagosa Springs. He was only here staying with his friend, Jack, to avoid his parents while he figured out how to tell them he'd decided not to go to college.

"Are you in a club?" Rachel nodded at a large 4-H club banner and lowered her eyes back to the dusty barn alley.

"No, not anymore. I graduated from high school last year. I don't actually live in La Plata County, anyway." Morgan shrugged.

"Oh? Where do you live then?" Rachel tied her steer to the pipe rail and ran a hand along his back, stopping to scratch the top of his tail.

"I grew up closer to Pagosa. My folks own Cross Creek Ranch over by Chimney Rock. You live close by?"

"On the mesa." Rachel picked up an empty bucket and started back down the alley.

"This your senior year?" Morgan walked along with her as she made her way to the water spigot.

She nodded. "Yep, and then I'm outta here."

His heart sank a little. She was leaving. He'd decided not to go to college because he loved it here so much. How could someone be so excited to leave?

She pushed down the valve handle and Morgan reached across to lift the heavy bucket before she could.

"Let me get this. You've earned a break." He chuckled and walked back to her spot in the market beef line-up and poured the water into the black rubber tub.

"Thanks." She was looking at him like he had three heads now.

She probably wondered why he was hanging around, but there was just something about her that intrigued him. Across the pavilion, a large banner reading La Plata County Fair Livestock Auction was being tacked to the front of the announcer's booth. Maybe she'd go to the dance with him after the sale tomorrow night.

Rachel opened a plywood box and pulled out a dusty plastic jug of lukewarm water.

"Wait." Morgan put a hand on her arm before she could take a drink. "Let's go get something *cold* to drink."

"I can't—" Rachel stumbled over her words.

"My treat."

She hesitated and wrapped her arms around herself, but shrugged. "Okay," she said. Her tone was uncertain, but the corner of her mouth quirked into the first smile he'd seen from her.

He nodded towards the cluster of food and drink vendors in the center of the festivities, and they walked out into the bright sunshine. "Sure is a hot day. I figured we'd be seeing some rain by now."

"Not yet." Rachel squinted to evaluate the bright blue Colorado sky. "It will, but probably not until tomorrow or Sunday."

"Oh really? You got the inside track on that from somewhere?" There wasn't a cloud in the sky.

Rachel laughed out loud, and the sound gripped him by the heart.

"It always rains—no—it always pours on Saturday night of fair week. The night of the sale." She nodded sagely. "That's when the monsoons will hit."

"That so?"

"Every time."

They ordered fresh-squeezed lemonade and fried pickles from a food truck with a bright yellow and green striped awning. Morgan motioned to the flashing lights and music behind the vendor booths. "Wanna go to the carnival?"

Rachel shrugged. "Not really my thing."

A group of girls stood in line at the tilt-a-whirl. One girl, in particular, was laughing and squealing loud enough to get the attention of everyone within a hundred yards of her. *Jessica.* Now, that could be a problem. Things with Jess had been over for a long time, but she'd never entirely released her claws from him. So if he took Rachel to the dance, would Jessica make things miserable for her?

"Come on." Rachel led the way, passing the livestock barns, and venturing into the trees that bordered the fairgrounds.

Just on the other side of the trees, the ground sloped sharply down to the railroad tracks, and on the other side, the Animas River glided by.

Rachel crossed the tracks and sat in the grass on the water's edge. Morgan sat down next to her and offered a paper cup salute before taking a drink of his lemonade.

"So, what is your story, then?" Rachel's eyes narrowed. Whether by the sun or just evaluating him, he didn't know. "What are you doing over here at our fair?"

"Honestly?" He grimaced, not sure even he knew the whole of it.

"Of course. Best policy, and all that." Her eyebrows rose as she took a long sip from her own cup.

He sighed. "Avoiding my folks."

"Is that so? Why? Are they awful or something?" Rachel turned her eyes to the river flowing swiftly by.

"Nah." He shook his head. "Actually, they're great."

Rachel blinked at him slowly and waited for an explanation rather than pushing.

"I'm supposed to leave for college in just a few weeks, but I've decided not to go. So, I'll be the first one of all my siblings not to go to college and make something of myself." He swallowed back the anxiety creeping up his throat. "I don't know how to tell them. I guess I'm not looking forward to disappointing two people who have worked so hard all their lives."

"So, you plan to be a hobo, is that it? Riding the rails of the D&SNG and panning for gold along the Animas?"

Morgan burst out laughing, allowing the tension building

inside him to release. "Well, no, of course not. I want to help my dad with the ranch. My family homesteaded that place nearly a hundred years ago. I just want to follow my heritage."

"I think that's pretty amazing. You have nothing to worry about. Your parents will be thrilled."

"I don't know. I've got some pretty big shoes to fill after everything my brothers and sister have done." Remembering the pickles, Morgan offered the paper tray to Rachel.

She picked out a few and popped one into her mouth. She sighed dreamily, closing her eyes.

"Wow, you really like those, don't you?" He smiled and took one for himself.

"My dad used to buy them for me every year." She braced her arms on her knees and stared into the water.

"And he doesn't anymore?" Morgan asked.

Rachel wiped a hand under her nose and shook her head. "He's gone. They're both gone."

Idiot. Way to go, Morgan.

His heart clenched. It was too late to take the comment back now. He might as well let her talk it out. "Can I ask what happened?"

Rachel chewed on the end of the straw for a long moment before answering. "Car accident four years ago."

"I'm so sorry. I didn't mean to—" Morgan faltered.

"It's okay. I never really get to talk about them to anyone. It's kinda nice." She gave him a weak smile.

"You don't live with family then?" He asked and ate another pickle, hoping the salt would ease the knot in his stomach.

She stopped before putting the pickle in her mouth and dropped her eyes. "No. We didn't have any family."

"So … you're in foster care?" He knew the drill. His parents had taken in countless kids from the foster system over the years. His mom always said it had been a way of reaching people.

Rachel frowned at the pickle in her hand. "The Johnsons." She tossed the fried treat into the water and rubbed her hands on her jeans. "At least they have a barn, so I was able to keep up with 4-H and had somewhere to keep Dante." She drew her knees up to her chest, hunkering behind them and resting her cheek on the denim.

"Dante?" Morgan asked.

"My horse. I couldn't leave him. I know it's silly, but he's all I have left."

She closed her eyes, and he brushed a thumb under her lashes. He wasn't sure what drove him to such an intimate gesture, but it was such a small thing when what he wanted to do was gather her up in his arms and hold her.

Rather than pull away from his touch, though, she pressed her cheek into the palm of his hand. Warmth, like a summer breeze, spread through him.

She reached up and rested her hand on his hand against her face. The sleeve of her shirt flapped open.

"I think you ripped your shirt during that escapade back there." Morgan laughed, but he noticed a blue bruise peeking through the ripped fabric as he reached for the tear.

Rachel jerked her hand back as though she'd been burned and crossed her arms against her chest.

"Did you hurt yourself? You have a bruise." He reached for her wrist but then held back, sensing the wall she'd just put up. "Rachel, are you okay?" His mouth went dry. Something wasn't right.

The sound of sliding gravel came from the trees on the hillside, and two cowboys stumbled out of the oak brush, laughing and shoving one another as they dug for something hidden in the bushes. Then, triumphant, one lifted a bottle overhead with a whoop.

Standing, Morgan helped Rachel to her feet. He should walk her back up to the fairgrounds. This was clearly not the place for a sweet girl like Rachel.

"Rachel?" One of the young men called out and attempted to hide the bottle behind his leg.

"Tate." A cherry red flush crept up Rachel's neck and face, and she crossed her arms as they walked up to meet the two others.

"What are you doing down here?" Tate's brow furrowed as he looked back and forth between Morgan and Rachel.

Did this guy have some kind of claim on her? She didn't seem overly excited to see him.

"Just hanging out. Tate, Brad, this is my friend Morgan." Rachel gave Morgan a sidelong look he couldn't quite read.

Tate's chest bowed out, and he ran his fingers down Rachel's arm, taking her hand. So that's how it was, huh? But rather than stepping closer to Tate, Rachel squirmed and pasted on a smile that was closer to a grimace.

"We'd better get going. I need to feed Sully and get home to do chores." Rachel pulled her hand out of Tate's and started back up the hill.

"See you at the dance," Tate called after them, but Rachel never looked back.

Morgan's mind wrestled with what had just happened. Were they a couple, or not? It sounded like they had plans to go to the dance together. Although she didn't seem all that happy about the prospect.

"He okay?" Morgan aimed a thumb over his shoulder as they walked back to the livestock pavilion.

"Tate?" Rachel shrugged. "Oh, sure. Just a guy from my 4-H club. He's been bugging me for a date for a while now. So, I said I'd go to the dance with him."

Did she not see the bottle behind Tate's back? But then again, maybe she didn't mind. Plenty of girls here were just as apt to drink and party, but something about how Tate had hidden that bottle told Morgan that she wasn't the partying type.

Should he say something? No. He'd probably just come off as jealous. Besides, between the problems Jessica could cause and the fact Rachel already had a date, Morgan better back off entirely.

CHAPTER 3

Rachel leaned against the cool rock wall outside the dance. All afternoon, thunderclouds had threatened to start the monsoon rains that came at this time of year, and she'd wondered if there would even be a dance. But, though storm clouds brewed dark overhead, the rain had stayed away, and the sale-night festivities had continued as planned.

Almost as planned, that is. The dance was well underway, and Rachel's date had yet to show up. She tapped the toe of her boot to the rhythm of the steel guitar. She probably should just go in without him, but dreaded the awkwardness of standing around alone.

Jessica Stanley and her gaggle were already inside, two-stepping to Randy Travis. Once she saw Morgan was Jessica's date to the dance, she had determined not to go in alone. She'd been humiliated enough after losing her steer and having to be rescued by Morgan. Then she'd gone all weepy when they'd spent the afternoon together. So embarrassing. She just couldn't suffer the indignation of seeing him face to face again with Jessica Stanley on his arm.

At least if she had a date of her own, she wouldn't look

quite so pathetic. Tate Newsome was hardly her type. He was one of the rowdier bunch in town, but this was her last year at the fair. She wanted at least one memory of her high school years that didn't involve the Johnson's filthy trailer house and the loneliness that had smothered her every day since losing her happy childhood. If that meant accepting any invitation to the dance that came her way, so be it. Besides, it was easier to go with someone that she had no desire to become attached to.

Where was Tate, anyway?

Laughter and singing carried on the breeze toward her from the direction of the beer tent. *Oh, no.* It wasn't—surely, he hadn't found someone to sneak drinks out—but yes, it was Tate, and yes, he and his buddies had been drinking.

Tate approached, howling at the moon. Rachel pushed off the wall she leaned against. Should she just leave? Clearly, this wasn't going to be the evening she'd had in mind.

"Rachel!" Tate hollered as she turned and headed for the parking lot. He grabbed her around the waist and swung her around in a circle. "Let's dance, schweetheart."

She pressed a hand into his chest and leaned back. "I don't think so. I'm going home."

"Awe, don't do that. Just one dance." Tate set her down, looking like a mournful puppy dog. "I'll behave, I promise."

She hesitated. Maybe it wouldn't be so bad. She at least wanted a few dances, and going in alone wasn't an option.

She allowed Tate to lead her into the courtyard-style space between the exhibit halls. Lights crisscrossed overhead, and couples circled the open area to the music being played by a DJ in the corner.

Tate pulled her into an upbeat two-step, swaying back and forth like a rocking horse and jerking their joined hands up and down. This was nothing like the smooth, gliding motion it had been when Dad used to dance with her in the kitchen.

Before her parents had died, she'd been too young to attend the dances. But Dad would often put an old record on and scoot the kitchen table out of the way, taking turns to dance with her and Mom. By the time she was old enough to go to the fair or street dances, her dad was gone. She'd give up every other dance for the rest of her life if she could just have one more night in the kitchen with him.

The song ended, and Rachel breathed a sigh of relief. She'd find an excuse to sit this next one out. Tugging her hand out of Tate's sweaty grasp and wiping her hand on her jeans, she jerked a thumb toward the concession stand.

"I'm going to get a drink," she shouted over the music. "Why don't you sit down for a minute?"

Tate stumbled back, and Rachel aimed his collapsing form onto a picnic table bench. She sighed and walked over to the concession stand, digging in the pocket of her jeans. She didn't have much. If she over-spent, she wouldn't be able to fuel her truck up for the drive back to the Johnson's.

The line moved forward, and she braced her arms on the cool metal of the order window.

"Can I just get a cup of ice water?" Rachel asked the woman behind the counter with an apologetic shrug.

"That'll be a quarter, sweetie. Unfortunately, we can't give the cups away for free."

"Yes, ma'am." She retrieved a quarter from her pocket and placed it down with a metallic clink on the counter.

The looming dark clouds and gentle breeze had lifted the oppressive heat of the day, but the cold water still soothed the lump in her throat. This night wasn't the night of memories she'd hoped it would be. Why on earth had she thought it might?

Tate was leaning back, sitting in the wrong direction on

the picnic table bench, hat askew, regaling his buddies with some tall tale. Rachel melted into the crowd. To be unseen and unheard wasn't hard for a wall-flower-nobody. Hopefully, Tate would forget all about their date, and she could simply stand aside and enjoy the music a while before going home.

Dancers passed in front of her, but one particular form caused her breath to catch in her chest. A faded purple t-shirt stretched across the unmistakable broad shoulders that could only belong to Morgan Cross. How could a guy like him pull off wearing that color? Truthfully, the purple faded nearly to a gray that contrasted nicely with his farmer's tan. Even if he was here with a girl Rachel despised, she couldn't help but be captivated by him.

When the dancing couples rounded the circle closer to her corner, Morgan's glance skimmed right over her. She shivered as goosebumps prickled her arms. Had he seen her? The dance carried him further across the room, and her chest tightened. What did it matter? He probably wouldn't notice her in the crowd. Even if he had, it wasn't like she'd made some great impression when they met. He probably saw her as the dumb girl who lost her steer and nearly wrecked the county fair.

She sat down on the concrete bench built into the rock wall and picked at the waxy Coca-cola logo on her water cup. Don Williams's "I Believe in You" came over the speaker, and a knot formed in her stomach. She set the cup aside. The water would do nothing to ease the thickness in her throat now.

It was the last song she and her father had danced to before he died. "I will always believe in you, Rachel," he had whispered down to the top of her head as they'd turned in slow circles on the linoleum floor. She would never forget that night. Mama had videotaped it, and it was the only tangible connection she had of them now that they were gone.

Tears rose to the surface, and she looked up, blinking rapidly to push them back. Was it getting late already, or were the darkening skies from thunderclouds rolling in? The darkness shadowed her, leaving her cold and empty.

A warmth penetrated the chill through her sleeve as someone sat close beside her on the bench. Sniffing, she turned and found Morgan looking down at her. How was it possible that the only two times in the past year or more she'd weakened to the point of tears, this guy had to be there to witness it?

"Dance with me." He smiled and nudged her arm.

"Oh, I shouldn't—" Rachel faltered. Why else would she be here? "I mean—it's just—I'm not a very good dancer."

She kicked herself for blurting it out, but what if she wasn't? Was dancing in the kitchen with her dad enough to keep her from making a fool of herself?

"Nonsense. All you need is a good partner."

He slipped his hand into hers, and with the slightest tension in his arm, she was carried away amid the dancing couples. Unlike the jerky, flailing motion of her dance with Tate, following Morgan's lead was effortless. He held her close, a firm hand supporting her back, and for the first time in four years, she felt secure.

They floated on the melody, and everything around them faded. The twinkling lights strung overhead reflected in Morgan's eyes, and the tickling of butterfly wings filled her chest. What would it be like to have a dance partner like Morgan to waltz her through the hard times? Was something like that even possible? No. Every good thing she'd ever had was taken from her. The song would end, and this moment would soon pass into distant memory.

And so it did. The music ended too soon, and when

Morgan spun her to a stop, Jessica was waiting on the edge of the dance floor, arms crossed. Rachel didn't even care. That single dance gave her the memory she'd been looking for, and she would hold on to it as long as she could.

"You're a terrific dancer, Rachel." Morgan's whisper tickled the top of her ear, and the sound of her name on his lips carried the tingling sensation down into the toe of her mama's old boots.

He gave her a wink and looked back over his shoulder at Jessica's rigid form. Huffing out a sigh, he squeezed Rachel's hand and turned around to speak to Jessica.

After what seemed like a brief argument, Morgan took Jessica's hand and twisted it around his back for a swing dance, disappearing into the crowded space. Rachel tucked a strand of hair behind her ear, and a smile lingered on her lips. She pressed them tight together to keep the sensation there as long as she could.

Regardless if Morgan was now dancing with someone else, she could go home happy. She had her moment, and that was all she could ask for.

Turning to leave, she walked straight into Tate's slanting form.

"There you are." His brows furrowed as he clutched her by the elbows. "I thought we were going to dance," he pouted.

"We danced, don't you remember?"

"Once."

Rachel's smile stiffened as she clenched her jaw. Why did her happy memory have to be tainted?

"Come on." Tate yanked her to the dance floor and started wildly swinging her around into pretzel shapes that weren't nearly as graceful as the other couples around them. Heat flushed into her cheeks as bystanders snickered at Tate's drunken antics.

When the song transitioned to a slow dance, she tried to slip from his grasp, but he pulled her in tight. Too tight. His breath reeked of yeasty beer, and every inch of her skin crawled as he pressed her to himself.

She didn't want to make a scene. Keeping her head turned, she braced herself to gain as much distance between them as possible. Then, when the music faded, she peeled herself free of him. He was like the leeches that clung to her legs when she played in mountain lakes as a girl.

"I'm going home, Tate," she insisted when he tried to grasp her hand again.

"No." He shook his head and tipped slightly sideways, stumbling as she pulled herself free.

"I'm going," she said, more forcefully this time. It was getting late anyway. She'd known she wouldn't have much time to stay at the dance, regardless. "Thanks for the date, but I'm going to be late for curfew." She enunciated the words, hoping he'd get the point.

She stepped out the side gate, refusing to linger any longer. He followed, and her stomach quivered. "Tate, I—"

"Newsome," someone shouted from the courtyard, derailing his attention.

Tate turned to shout animated epithets to his intoxicated friend, and Rachel jogged toward her truck. Why did such a perfect memory like her dance with Morgan have to be tarnished by a clingy drunk? *Story of my life.*

She climbed into the truck and turned the key. *Click-click-click-click.* No. Oh, please God, no. She tried again. *Click-click.*

"Argh!" She slammed her hand against the steering wheel and stepped back out of the truck, pulling the lever to release the hood latch. It was the battery again.

Pulling the seat forward, she pulled out the set of jumper cables. Surely someone would be out in the parking lot soon, and she could get a jump. She shut the truck door harder than necessary and turned to see if anyone was near.

"Where'd you go?" Tate's slurred speech greeted her before she even saw him.

She turned to rebuff him, but he kissed her hard, smashing her lips against her teeth as he pushed her against her truck. This could not be happening.

Pushing him away, she kneed him in the groin with all her strength. He instinctively bent down, and she slammed her knee into his face, sending him toppling over onto the asphalt. Drunk as he was, he should be down long enough for her to get away.

She yanked her keys from the ignition, stepped over the limp form on the ground, and headed straight for the highway.

What next, God?

A crack of thunder answered overhead, and a raindrop landed on her cheek. She sighed. It was going to be a long walk home.

CHAPTER 4

Morgan turned up the radio and gripped the steering wheel tight. The windshield wipers worked at full speed, barely keeping up with the downpour. His arms were heavy with the weight of his lost chance.

He'd only taken Jess out on the dance floor to appease her. She'd been mad as a wet hen, just like he'd thought she'd be, and the last thing he wanted for a quiet girl like Rachel was to be pounced on by a predator like his ex. But when he'd finished the swing number with Jess, Mrs. Hilgar, an old family friend, had insisted on the next song. By the time he'd found himself free again, Rachel was nowhere to be seen.

He turned onto the county road and muddy water splashed against his window from a large puddle. Maybe it was for the best. He shouldn't allow himself to be distracted right now. He needed to get home and level with his folks that he would not be going to CSU after all.

He'd crash at Jack's place one more night, then head home tomorrow. With two brothers already graduated from college, and a sister on her way to becoming a veterinarian, he hated the idea of being the disappointment in the family by not continuing his education.

The truth was, his dreams had never been to go to school or find a career that would take him away from the ranch. Ranching was the life he loved, and he wanted nothing more than to continue the family's legacy.

Five generations of his family had worked and thrived on that piece of ground, raising everything from Suffolk sheep to Hereford cattle. If he went off to school, all he'd be doing would be spending unnecessary money on a piece of paper. Sure, there was more he could learn. He wasn't so arrogant to think he wouldn't benefit from school, but he'd rather learn hands-on from Dad than go to the extra time and expense.

The colorful glare of streetlights and stop lights faded as he turned down the county road that led to Jack's house. He hadn't waited around for his friend to want to head home. Once he'd realized Rachel was gone, he'd lost interest in the dance.

Though it was still raining, visibility cleared without the blurring of lights from town, and he eased back in the seat. His headlights cast a ray through the deluge, illuminating a feminine form on the shoulder of the road. He pulled up ahead of her and stopped the truck. It wasn't his habit to pick up hitchhikers, but he couldn't possibly leave someone out in this gully washer. Morgan leaned across the bench seat and opened the door when the woman appeared in the side mirror.

"Hop in!" he raised his voice over a clap of thunder.

His heart skipped faster when Rachel, soaked to the bone, climbed into the passenger seat.

"What the heck are you doing out in this mess?" Morgan pulled his hoodie over his head and held it out to her.

"Tr-truck wouldn't start." Her voice caught as she shivered into the dry sweatshirt.

"And you couldn't find someone to give you a ride? What about your date?" He couldn't keep the steel out of his tone.

He knew why she hadn't ridden home with Tate. He'd seen the idiot stumbling drunk in the parking lot, his shirt stained from the remnants of a bloody nose from a fight. There was no way Morgan would've squandered a date with someone like Rachel by showing up three sheets to the wind.

"I didn't have anybody to ask. Riding home with Tate was not an option." An undercurrent of disdain reverberated under her flat tone.

"You could've asked me." Morgan gave her a half-smile, uncertain why she wouldn't have at least asked before walking all this way. She must've hitchhiked part of the way, far as she was from the fairgrounds.

"I didn't want to mess up your date." Rachel tucked her hands into the sleeves and wrapped her arms around herself.

"Date?" He frowned as he turned the heater vent toward her. "I didn't have a date tonight."

Rachel's eyebrows raised. "I saw you with Jessica Stanley."

Morgan stifled a groan. Would his past mistake of dating that girl ever stop haunting him?

"She was not my date. Not tonight anyway." He gripped the steering wheel tight.

"What'd you mean, not tonight?" Rachel poked her hands out of the sleeves to warm them in front of the heater vent, stretching her fingers and closing her eyes in apparent bliss.

"We dated last year, but she's not been keen to let things go. We hang out with some of the same people, so she's somewhat unavoidable at times." Fog crept across the windshield, and he turned the heater back to the defroster with an apologetic look.

"She sure seemed upset when we were dancing." Rachel tucked her hands back in and shivered.

"Which is the only reason I danced with her. To get her off your back." Morgan grimaced. It sounded like a pretty lame excuse once he said it out loud. "You can come over here and warm up. I promise no biting and no funny business." He put his arm on the back of the seat and raised his eyebrows in question.

She hesitated. He couldn't blame her, but the poor girl looked miserable.

"Your lips are purple." He reached out and unthreaded the heavy Darth Vader gearshift knob. "Here," he offered it to her. "If I turn into a sleazeball, you can crack me in the head with this." He winked, hoping to ease her apprehension.

A flicker of a smile tucked in at the corner of her vibrating lips. "Alright, but I'll warn you, it won't be the first broken nose I've handed out tonight if you do." Her shoulders shook with suppressed laughter.

Realization dawned on Morgan. "Tate? No way. That was you?" Thoroughly impressed and slightly unnerved, he rested his arm on the seat-back again.

Weighing the shifter knob in her palm, she gave him a sidelong glance before unbuckling and scooting over beside him, tucking under his arm. An electric current sent a shock wave to his heart. She fit perfectly, nestled against him. He drew in an intentionally slow breath, hoping to calm his frantic heart rate. After promising not to be a sleazeball, the last thing he needed was for her to hear his heart pounding through his t-shirt.

"Better?" he asked as her shivering slowed.

"Definitely. It's like you've got a heater under there." She laughed, and the easy sound filled the empty feeling in his chest.

"Mom always said I was her personal heater when I was

little." He rested his arm across her back. "Where are we headed, by the way?"

"County Road 223." She lifted her head to look out the windshield. "Second driveway on the right."

"So, this is a foster family?" Morgan drummed the steering wheel with his left hand to the beat of the music. "How's that been?"

Rachel shrugged under his arm. "Fine, I guess."

That wasn't good. With the kids that had come through his house growing up, he had always thought they were pretty happy at the ranch. No doubt they were frustrated by their situation, but his folks always made sure they felt as secure as possible. But not every foster situation was so ideal.

"You must be near eighteen, though."

Rachel nodded. "Three months." She sighed. "Three months, one week, and four days."

"That's rather specific." Morgan laughed a humorless laugh. Why was she counting down the days? That didn't sit well with him.

"We're here." Rachel sat bolt upright. "Stop the truck."

"We're not at the house yet." His stomach knotted at her sudden change of demeanor.

"Good. Can you kill the lights?" She peeled the sweatshirt over her head. "I'll walk from here."

"What are you talking about? It's still dumping out there."

"I'm good, thanks." Her hand trembled as she reached for the door handle.

The hairs on the back of Morgan's neck rose, and he reached out, gently resting it on her shoulder. "Are you going to be okay?"

"Yeah, I'll be fine." Rachel inflated her lungs like they might float her the rest of the way to the house.

"Hey, wait. How can I get a hold of you?" His guts were

churning now. Something felt off. "Can I at least call and make sure you didn't die of pneumonia?"

"Better not," she said, shaking her head.

Morgan's shoulders slumped with the weight of her response. Maybe she just wasn't interested.

"Cross Creek Ranch?" She perked up a little.

"Yeah."

"Maybe I'll look you up in three months, one week, and four days." Her attempted wink faltered into a rapid blinking, but before he could stop her, she jumped out and ran up the driveway to the house.

Morgan waited at the driveway entrance to make sure she made it in the house alright. The trailer house was mostly dark, with only a flickering light showing through the front window. Rachel lifted a corner of the doormat and removed a key. She unlocked the door and replaced the key, slipping inside.

He turned the truck around at the driveway entrance. Maybe he was just jumpy? A light switched on in the house, shining in his rear-view mirror as he pulled back onto the county road. Something inside him, a quiet voice but much more significant than his own, told him to go back. He stopped the truck and rolled the window down. The unmistakable sound of shouting came from the house, layered over the rain drumming on the windshield.

He slammed the truck into reverse, and gravel flew out from under his tires as he watched the house growing more prominent in the mirror. *God, help me help her.* His silent plea coursed through his humming veins as he jumped out of the truck and ran for the house.

CHAPTER 5

Rachel replaced the key under the mat and turned the doorknob silently, slipping inside. The light from the TV glowed in the dark living room. *Please, God, let them be asleep.* Tom often passed out in his chair watching old episodes of *Gunsmoke*.

"Where you been, girl?" Tom Johnson's slurring voice sent a shudder down her spine.

The fear rushing through her veins was far colder than her rain-soaked clothes. A light flipped on, and she blinked rapidly to gain her bearings.

"My truck broke down. I had to walk." Rachel backed into the corner of the room.

"Liar." The crackling rasp of Cathy's voice raked over Rachel's nerves. Cathy slumped against the refrigerator door, peering at Rachel through one open eye. "You been out foolin' around when you oughta be here taking care of your chores. You know you got a ten o'clock curfew. Ain't no excuses."

"But my truck …" Rachel's feeble response trailed off.

There was no point in trying to explain—they wouldn't

listen. Tom stood from his chair and stumbled toward Rachel. She crouched in the corner and held her arm over her head in defense. White-hot pain shot up her wrist as Tom's beefy hand grabbed her and wrenched her wrist, jerking her into the middle of the room.

She clutched the arm to her chest and bunched her shoulders around her ears. With nothing to shield her now, she'd just have to take it blow by blow. Tom picked up a phone book and rolled it.

"Please don't. I'm sorry," she cried out. Why hadn't she gotten away before tonight?

"Stop your screeching, girl," Cathy called out, slamming the door of the cupboard containing their collection of alcohol.

They must be on the tequila tonight. It was always worse when it was tequila. Rachel bit her lip to quiet the moan that threatened to escape her. He might have broken the wrist this time.

Tom raised the rolled-up phone book high and brought it down over the top of her head, jarring her neck and sending a shock wave down her spine. Cold nausea flooded her, and she dropped to the dingy carpet liberally dusted with cigarette ash. She curled into a ball, protecting her wrist.

The front door flew open, banging into the cluttered end table. Crumpled beer cans scattered across the floor with a clatter.

"What the—" Tom's outcry was cut short as Morgan slammed into him like an angry bull against a gate.

Cathy cowered behind the kitchen counter, blubbering. Rachel scrambled to her feet and wavered, her vision speckled with white stars. She leaned against the wall. Her head was splitting, and her wrist burned like hellfire.

Emotions warred in her like the wrestling match on the living room floor. Relief to have her unspoken prayers answered and worry that Morgan would get hurt all tumbled around inside her.

The turmoil in front of her stopped, and Morgan slammed a knee into Tom's back, bringing both Tom's wrists up behind him.

"Can you get my belt?" Morgan spoke for the first time, his voice tight with strain.

Rachel dropped to her knees, cringing as the bones of her wrist grated when she landed.

She used her left hand to unbuckle Morgan's belt and pull it free from the belt loops. Morgan took the belt and secured Tom's hands and feet together in a hog-tie.

"She gonna be a problem?" Morgan shot a glance back over his shoulder as he secured the belt.

Rachel shook her head. The woman wailed incoherently from her hiding place, like a deranged alley cat.

"We're getting out of here." Morgan's look of disgust sent a rush of blood to her face. Having him here, in this filthy house, witnessing how she'd been living was humiliating.

"I can't." Rachel shook her head, defeated. "Dante—my horse—the Johnson's were the only ones who would let me keep him." She slumped as the renewed weight of her situation settled back on her shoulders.

"We'll figure that out later. Right now, we're getting you out of this place." Morgan smoothed a large hand over her hair and lifted her chin. "Pack your bag. I'm calling the police." He helped her up by her good elbow and pointed her in the direction of the hallway.

A sinking feeling settled in her stomach as she retreated to the bedroom to pack. She should be elated right now, but the fear of losing Dante battled with her desperation to leave this place and never look back.

Sully had sold this weekend, so he wasn't going to be a concern, but what if no other foster families were willing or able to take her *and* her horse? Rachel opened the black trash bag one-handed and hung it on a coat hook in the closet. She rested one hand on her denim chore coat and hesitated. Was this the right thing to do?

She stuffed her things into the bag and, exhausted, slumped onto the bed. Her head pounded—she was so tired. Maybe she could just lay here for a few minutes. With Morgan in the living room, Rachel was confident the Johnson's wouldn't be coming in to retaliate.

She dozed in and out of sleep until red and blue flashing lights flooded the house. Sitting up, she pulled the tattered curtain to the side and watched as a Sheriff's Department Jeep Cherokee pulled into the drive. She swallowed against the dryness in her mouth and stuffed her clothes into the bag with one hand. Was Morgan right? Should she go?

∾

MORGAN PUNCHED the keypad to the hospital vending machine with force, and the bottle of soda dropped with a clatter. It might as well have hit the bottom of his stomach rather than the vending machine for the way his guts ached. Would Rachel tell the truth? He wasn't so sure.

He didn't think she would be out to get him into any trouble, but it was also clear she wasn't sure about the idea of leaving the Johnson's house. While the EMTs had looked at her wrist and the sheriff's deputies assessed the scene, Rachel had been agitated—saying over and over, "they're going to take him, they're going to take Dante."

When the CPS officer asked Morgan to leave the curtained emergency room cubby, Rachel had mouthed, "I'm sorry."

What had she meant? Sorry Morgan had been dragged into this mess or sorry for whatever she was about to tell

CPS? Would she suffer through another three months of abuse just to make sure she could keep her horse?

Morgan leaned against the wall and cracked the lid to the Dr. Pepper open with a fizzing escape of carbonation. He didn't even taste the liquid as it went down, but it wet his dry mouth and soothed the ache in his throat.

That Johnson woman had told the cops he had attacked her husband and knocked Rachel over in the process—breaking Rachel's wrist. Mrs. Johnson was good. He had to admit it. She'd collected herself when the deputies knocked at the door and showed little sign of drunkenness. But so far, the evidence must support his story because they'd arrested Tom and allowed Morgan to accompany Rachel to the hospital.

Morgan prayed Rachel would ask to be removed from the Johnson's home and that his folks would get here in time. Even if they found someone to place Rachel with, would he ever see her again? Who knows where she would end up if his plan didn't work out?

He'd called his parents as soon as he'd reached the hospital and asked them to bring the horse trailer. It was the only solution he could think of that might convince Rachel not to go back. However, the flurry of nurses and interruption of the CPS officer had kept him from telling her his plan.

"Morgan?" The familiar voice came from the waiting area.

His mom, obviously too impatient to wait at the nurse's desk, was looking around the room, calling his name. He released a huge breath and strode across the black and white tile floor, unashamed to pull her to him in a hug.

"Dad dropped me off." Mom forced the words out past his crushing embrace. "He's parking the truck and will be right in. Do you want to tell me just what's going on here?"

He took her by the hand and slumped into a chair. "I don't even know where to start." He released her hand and pressed his palms against his eyes.

"You can start with who this girl is and why you were at her house at eleven o'clock at night."

"Mom."

"I know, I know, you're not technically living under our roof anymore." Mom waved a hand in dismissal. "But I certainly hope you had a good reason." She narrowed her eyes, and Morgan's shoulders shook with repressed laughter.

All the weight of tension had lifted now that his folks were here. Randy and Maggie Cross had been working with CPS and taking in foster children for ten years. If anyone knew how to help Rachel, it would be them.

"She's a girl I met this week at the fair." Morgan sighed. "I was on my way to Jack's house after the dance tonight, and she was walking down the county road."

"In the rain?" Mom's forehead scrunched.

"In a downpour," he continued. "Her truck broke down, and her date was drunk. And apparently, she was so terrified of missing her curfew. She attempted to walk eight miles home in the rain."

"Where are her parents?" Mom looked around the waiting area.

"Passed on. She's a foster kid, Mom." Morgan leveled a serious look at his mom, and she nodded slowly. "I dropped her off, but something didn't feel right. I heard shouting, so I went back. When I got to the door, the jerk had already broken her wrist."

"Oh, no." Mom blinked rapidly and covered her mouth. "Some people are only in it for the monthly check. It's a shame when someone like that gets through the cracks of the system. Most really just want to help."

The automatic doors parted, and a John Wayne look-alike walked through, eyeing the room with a narrow glare. Morgan stood, catching Dad's eye, and nodded. When Dad sat down next to Mom, the knot in Morgan's stomach loosened a bit more.

He caught Dad up with as little detail as possible, "Foster girl, a new friend. Folks were abusive, and I got her out of there."

Dad nodded. He wouldn't need any additional explanation.

"I hog-tied the jerk and called the sheriff." Morgan finished the rundown of the evening's activities.

"You what?" Mom shrieked, eliciting a glare from the nurse at the nurse's station. Dad nodded in approval.

"Well, what else was I supposed to do?"

"That's all just fine, son, but just where do we come into all this?" Dad leaned back and pressed his hands against his knees.

"She won't leave." Morgan leaned forward, bracing his elbows on his knees. "She doesn't want to be placed in a new home because she only has three months left, and these folks had means to keep livestock. She's got a horse.

"Horse people." Dad rolled his eyes playfully.

Morgan smothered a chuckle. "She's not *that* kind of horse person, Dad. She's really down to earth. It's just this horse ties her to her life before." He shrugged.

"Well, of course, we'll help, won't we, Randy?" Mom batted her eyes expertly at her husband, and Morgan looked at the floor, hiding a grin.

When he had graduated high school, his folks had stopped taking in new kids. But with Mom flashing doe eyes at Dad, there was no question they would help Rachel if they could.

The CPS officer exited the curtained area where Rachel was, and Morgan's parents stood and met her halfway.

"Sandy," Mom greeted the tired-looking woman by name.

Sandy Brinkman looked up, eyes wide, but smiled through her fatigue.

"Maggie Cross, what are you doing here?"

"I wondered if you had a few minutes."

Morgan's gut twisted into a half-hitch while he waited. Would this even work? Would CPS allow his parent's unconventional proposal to take Rachel themselves?

Morgan rested his elbows on his knees again and pressed his clenched hands against his forehead. "God, please," he whispered. "Please help her." He repeated the prayer, over and over, with every heartbeat until Mom returned with the news.

CHAPTER 6

The hollow musical notes of a wind chime pulled Rachel to the surface of consciousness. Morning light gleamed through a prism that dangled in front of the window, sending a shower of rainbow light dancing around the room. She lay on a bed piled with blankets and pillows, surrounded in comfort, and her casted arm rested on a pillow beside her.

Painful wrist or not, she hadn't been this at peace since her parents died. She drew in a languid breath and stretched, careful not to move the injured arm. The room had a definite denim and lace vibe going on, with posters of horses on the walls. It was just the sort of thing she would have wanted if she still had the life she was born to. The name "Katie" stretched across the wall in raised, hand-painted letters. Morgan's sister, maybe?

She still couldn't fathom what had happened the night before. The last thing she'd wanted was to go back to the Johnsons' house, but for the sake of keeping Dante, she would have endured another three months. She'd no idea where she would have gone after moving out, but she'd have been willing to find a grassy park up a forest service road and live out of her truck if it meant being free. At least then, she'd be a legal adult and less likely to run into trouble as a runaway and have Dante taken from her.

She had thought staying with the Johnson's would be her only option until she turned eighteen. She had told the social worker the broken wrist was an accident, resigned to stick things out. Instead, when the nurse pulled back the curtain to discharge her, a couple who turned out to be Morgan's parents were speaking to Ms. Brinkman.

Morgan's mom was standing with her back turned, but Rachel heard her clear as day, "We don't care about the check from the state. All we care about is giving this sweet young woman a safe place to live and a fresh start when she's ready to move out."

She still wasn't sure she would believe it had all happened if it wasn't for the soft blankets practically smothering her or the savory essence of bacon wafting in through the open crack of the bedroom door. Her stomach rumbled at the scent of breakfast, reassuring her that this was no dream. Nevertheless, she couldn't quite bring herself to climb out from between the smooth sheets just yet. Closing her eyes, she sank back into the depths of the fluffy pillow. Maybe just a few more minutes of sleep.

∽

MORGAN HOPPED out of his truck and sank ankle-deep. The rain the night before had left the ranch a mud bog. He'd barely gotten his truck up to the main house without putting it in 4-low. Now that he was sure he'd stay put and not go off to CSU, he would need to get a load of gravel down on his driveway this fall, or he'd never leave the back forty come winter. That was if Dad agreed to his proposal.

Morgan had been staying in the old homestead cabin on

the back of their property all summer. It was only meant to be temporary, a way to have his own space after graduating high school. But now it was time to level with his folks that he had no intention of going to college and make an offer to buy the cabin from them.

He knocked briefly before walking in, scraping the mud from his irrigation boots on the grate by the back door.

"Morning," he announced himself, and sat down on the wooden chair by the door.

"Boots." Mom's voice carried from the kitchen on a wave of frying bacon and strong, black coffee.

"They're off." Morgan pulled his boots off and set them next to a worn pair of women's Ropers. So, she was here. What a whirlwind last night had been. This morning, he had nearly thought it'd all been a wild dream until Mom called to tell him they'd be staying home from church today while Rachel rested up and settled in.

Rachel. The thrill of her name sent a hot-shot jolt straight to his heart. That girl was something else. Strong as a 1,500-pound steer, and by all accounts, he'd seen, just as stubborn. She'd been willing to tough it out in that awful trailer house, being used and abused just to make sure she could keep her horse. Most of the foster kids they'd taken in over the years had gone through a rude awakening with the hard work that came with farm life, but Rachel would fit in just fine.

Morgan walked into the kitchen and kissed Mom on the cheek before snagging a cup of coffee. He added a sizable slug of heavy cream and a tablespoon of sugar. He needed all the help he could get this morning.

The table was set for four, but Rachel was nowhere in sight. He didn't want to seem too eager, so he bit back the questions burning on his tongue like scalding coffee. Was she okay? Where did they put her up? Surely not in his old room. Something about that idea seemed far too intimate, though he couldn't say why.

"Dad still doing chores?" He should've checked the barn before he came to the house.

"He's just washing up." Mom wiped her hands on a dishtowel and poured orange juice into four small glasses.

Morgan nodded and leaned against the kitchen counter, tucking his hands into his pockets.

Mom twisted her lips in a knowing smile. "Rachel's still in bed. I reckon she'll be needing some extra sleep with the night she had."

"You're gonna let her sleep?" He wasn't sure he'd ever been allowed to sleep past seven in the morning his entire life. But then again, he hadn't ever been through what Rachel had been through for the past four years.

Mom just cocked her head and handed him two glasses of orange juice. "I reckon it's reasonable for her to sleep clean through to next week after the time she's had." Mom's stern voice echoed his thoughts as she set down the other two glasses.

"Somethin' smells mighty fine this morning." Dad's baritone echoed off the high rafter ceiling.

"Lower your voice, Randy." Mom raised her eyebrows and whispered, pointing down the hall.

Dad's forehead bunched, bringing dark eyebrows together like two furry caterpillars. "You gonna let her sleep all day?"

Mom rolled her eyes and poured Dad a cup of coffee. "Aren't you a pair?"

Dad looked over at Morgan and shrugged, mumbling to Morgan, "What'd we do now?"

Morgan chuckled and shook his head. He had an uncomplicated relationship with his folks. So, why did it make the cream curdle in his stomach at the thought of telling them he wasn't going to college this fall? Maybe because he'd be the first of four kids not to go? Because they'd been so proud of all his siblings and their accomplishments, that was why. One brother was now a geological engineer, another a water conservation specialist, and his sister, a future veterinarian. How could he tell them he just wanted to be a rancher?

He sighed and went to join his parents at the large dining table.

"We'll go ahead and eat. Rachel needs all the rest she can get." Dad announced as though it was his idea in the first place. "Even if no one asked me if I wanted to sleep late," Dad murmured and winked at Morgan, bowing his head. "Lord, we thank you for the food on our table and the love in this house. I pray we can be a blessing to that sweet girl down the hall. Amen."

"You already have." A soft voice came from behind Morgan.

Rachel stepped tentatively out of the hallway, fidgeting with the end of her messy braid. Glittering rays of light poured in through the picture window of the dining room, casting a glow over her. She wore a t-shirt that was three sizes too big and a pair of plaid shorts.

He'd seen nothing so beautiful. His throat went dry. Darting his eyes to the table-top, he grabbed the glass of orange juice in front of him and choked as the acidic pulp seemed to get lodged in his throat. Coughing and sputtering into his napkin, he resisted the urge to crawl under the table.

"Oh, darlin', come have a seat." Mom jumped up and guided Rachel to the seat across from Morgan.

She sat back down and passed the biscuits over to Rachel, whose eyes lit up like she'd been handed a basket of gold nuggets and not bread.

She pinched off a piece and closed her eyes in rapture as she took a bite. "These are amazing."

"Did your mama like to cook?" Mom asked, careful to focus on happier memories rather than the past four years.

"Mm-hmm." Rachel nodded and took two slices of bacon as Mom handed her the platter.

"Did she teach you?"

"A little." Rachel blinked rapidly, but the brightness of her eyes made his heart clench.

"Well then, we'll just have to get you in the kitchen and get you cooking some good down-home food then. You look like you could use it." Mom smiled and pushed the butter dish toward Rachel.

"I'd like that." Rachel returned the smile and picked up her biscuit to butter it.

The table fell silent as everyone ate.

"So—" Dad liberally buttered his own biscuit and pointed the butter knife in Morgan's direction—"when do you take off for CSU then, son?"

Morgan took a long swallow of coffee, his chest tightening. "Umm, well …" he hesitated. How was he going to convince them this was the right thing for him?

Rachel widened her eyes at him from across the table and kicked him with her bare foot. Sighing, he straightened his shoulders and lifted his chin. Rachel had been right the other day. He had a loving family, and he didn't have a reason to be so apprehensive.

"About that"—Morgan set the coffee cup down and looked from Mom to Dad —"I'm not." He darted a glance over at Rachel, who gave him an encouraging smile.

"Oh?" Mom glanced at Dad and back to Morgan.

"I've put a lot of thought into this. I know how proud you've been to have all your kids going to school and doing big things." He drummed his fingers restlessly on the oak dining table. "But the truth is, that's just not what I want."

"And just what is it you want?" Dad lowered a caterpillar eyebrow.

"This." Morgan waved a hand at the pasture full of cattle out the window. "I want to help you with the ranch. I can either stay on and take over things when the time comes or buy out some of it now. I can use the money I've saved up for college."

As quiet as the room became, a strand of hay would've sounded like a boulder if it dropped to the floor. His folks shared a long look. What if they said no? What if they were so upset they wouldn't sell him the cabin and the back forty or allow him to take over? If he wasn't ranching the family homestead, would he even want to ranch?

"Thank heavens." Mom was the first to break the stoic exchange between his folks. She glanced back at Dad, who chuckled.

What was happening? Were they really okay with this?

"We knew college wasn't the right fit for you." Dad finally spoke up. "We wanted you to make your own choice—not feel pressured to stay—but you're at your best here on the ranch, not in a classroom or an office somewhere." Dad patted Morgan's hand. "Besides, this ranch has been in the family for six generations. If you chose not to stay, who would we pass all this heritage down to?"

Allowing his head to fall back, Morgan sent up a silent prayer of thanksgiving for his family. All the turmoil he'd been going through was purely self-inflicted.

He let out a huge breath and slumped back in his chair, meeting Rachel's eye across the table. She grinned and mouthed a silent "told you so." The weight on his chest lifted. Everything seemed to be falling into place.

CHAPTER 7

Rachel walked beside Morgan through the upper pasture. The tall grass that hadn't been grazed this summer now laid over into a brown mat on the cold ground. A cool breeze nipped at her arms, and a flurry of crackly oak leaves whipped around them.

She rubbed her arms to generate some heat. Morgan stopped and unbuttoned his quilted flannel shirt, wrapping it around her. "I told you to grab a jacket."

She slipped her arms in the sleeves, and Morgan's lingering warmth sent a tingle down to her toes. "But now you're going to be cold."

She bunched her fists in the cuffs and rubbed his arms below the sleeve of his t-shirt.

"I'll survive." He winked and snapped the buttons of the shirt for her. A gaze lingered between them, and suddenly, she no longer needed the extra layer. Heat climbed up her neck and into her cheeks. She brought her flannel-covered hands up to her face to hide the blush that must be glowing like a summer tomato.

Morgan turned and leaned an elbow on a weathered

fence post. This section of property hadn't been used for livestock in years, and the barbed wire fence had long since fallen into disrepair. Morgan's section now, it had been a part of the original homestead. The empty meadow consisted of a few acres of flat ground surrounded by large pinion trees. It was higher in elevation than the main house he'd grown up in and overlooked the rest of the Cross family's property.

"It's beautiful up here." Rachel looked down at the broad expanse of mountain scenery below.

"This was my favorite spot growing up." Morgan smiled proudly.

Red and orange oak brush blanketed the rolling hills below, surrounding hundreds of acres of pasture stretched out across the valley. Feeling their oats from the new chill in the air, the horses bucked and ran through the horse pasture to the south. Dante nipped at Maggie's black mare as she ran past him. Even Dante had gained a healthier sheen to his coat. He was getting downright fat and sassy. All of this was so surreal.

Cross Creek Ranch no longer felt like a temporary home. In the past couple of months, she had a sense of family again. Maggie and Randy treated her like a daughter. Unlike the endless labor she'd experienced before, the chores she did now were rewarding and energizing. The work gave her a sense of purpose and belonging.

Most recently, Rachel and Maggie had been harvesting the garden and had canned what seemed like hundreds of jars of pickles, salsa, and green beans. Enough to feed them all winter—all year, really—with hardly any need to go to the store.

The breath caught in her chest as though a horse had kicked her. She wouldn't be here this winter. In another month, she would turn eighteen and would need to find a new place to stay. Not that the Cross's had said anything about her leaving, but they'd only taken her in to ensure she and Dante would have a safe place until she was a legal adult. It wouldn't be right for her to impose on their generosity any longer than necessary.

Tears prickled behind her lashes, and she turned her face, wiping away the wetness and hoping Morgan wouldn't notice. As she dried her eyes, the sun was disappearing over the mountains in the west.

"Wow," she whispered shakily, willing the tears to stay in place.

A red and yellow haze glowed behind the treetops below a blanket of dark blue. Who knew where she would be in a few months? Would she even be able to stay in Colorado? She couldn't say.

"When I build my house up here, I'm going to have two-story windows all along this side of the house," Morgan spoke over her shoulder. His breath tickled the tip of her ear, and a shiver ran down to her toes.

"Oh?" Rachel turned to see Morgan's face, bringing their faces just a few inches apart. She held her breath, unable to move.

His fingertips grazed her arm through the flannel fabric of his shirt.

"Would you like that?" Morgan asked.

His voice was barely above a whisper now. His eyes bored a hole into hers and filled them with some magic that held her motionless. He picked a crackling oak leaf from her shoulder and tucked her hair behind her ear.

"What do you mean?"

Surely he couldn't intend what she was hearing.

"Would you like to have big windows facing that sunset every night?"

Her heart flipped in her chest like the fluttering of fall

leaves. She'd wanted nothing so much in all her life. Wouldn't that be jumping the gun a bit? They hadn't even dated, not really.

Sure, they'd spent countless hours together these past few months. Horse rides in the mountains, movie nights, and popcorn fights on the couch. He'd become her best friend since she'd moved in with his folks. But she hadn't dared to dream it was anything more. After all, this was no Cinderella story, was it?

"You can't mean—Morgan, what are you saying?" She needed to be sure before letting herself dare to believe.

Morgan tipped her chin, and his eyes lingered on her lips. Her heart raced like the horses running through the field below. He bent his head slowly and threaded his fingers through her hair, grazing her lips in a light caress. When she opened her eyes, the sun had set, and the shadow of the mountain blanketed them in darkness.

"Will you let me build you a house right here next summer?" His fingers slid down the back of her neck, and he nudged her nose with his own. With the growing dark hiding his expression, his every touch sent electricity flying down every nerve.

"Only if you promise to clean those two-story windows yourself." Rachel chuckled, and he pressed his forehead against hers, shaking with laughter.

Morgan wrapped firm hands behind her back and pulled her closer. She leaned in instinctively, and he hesitated. The anticipation of kissing him again built in her chest like a fire being kindled. He kissed her in earnest now, fanning the flames. His lips were firm yet tender and set her heart fully ablaze. Her lips melted into his, and goosebumps skittered up her neck in a shower of sparks. Nothing had ever felt so right before. When he finally pulled away and stepped back, she opened her eyes. Morgan was gone.

Rachel looked around frantically in the dark. Had he vanished into thin air? Maybe he'd passed out from all the excitement. She looked down and found him, not swooning from her exceptional first kiss mojo but standing about two feet shorter than her now. He'd stepped back in the dark and fallen in an old post hole.

Shaking with laughter, he grabbed her by the legs and toppled her over on the grass beside him. He climbed out of the hole and laid down next to her, threading his fingers through hers. As they lay under the emerging stars, a sense of peace and certainty settled over her like a warm quilt.

This was home now and always would be. It was okay to be happy. Life on Cross Creek Ranch was what her parents would have wanted for her. They wouldn't want her to be buried in grief, barely living a stagnant life. They would want her to live a full life and to thrive.

She squeezed Morgan's hand and snuggled against his shoulder. Who would have thought she would find love and new life at the county fair?

EPILOGUE

Morgan glided the rubber scraper edge over the window in a slow, careful line. No wonder Rachel had demanded that he would be the one to keep these windows clean. The way the sun poured in over the mountain tops in the evening was a remarkable sight, but it also highlighted every spot and blemish when they weren't clean. She had her hands full enough without worrying about the floor-to-ceiling windows, too.

Just then, Rachel walked into the kitchen with a round-faced, tow-headed boy on her hip. Morgan watched through the glass as she deposited him into a highchair and set a colorful sippy cup in front of him.

Morgan lowered the squeegee to the ground below him and gripped the edges of the metal ladder tight. How was it he'd gotten here? Not long ago, he'd been bound for college, trapped in a future he hadn't wanted. Now, three years later, he was running the ranch with Dad and had a wife and family of his own. It was so much more than he'd ever dreamed of.

He descended the ladder and carried the bucket to the

house. Inside, country music played over the radio on the kitchen counter, and the warm, buttery scent of fresh-baked biscuits filled the air.

"Smells good in here," Morgan said as he deposited the bucket of sudsy water in the mud-room.

He slipped off his boots and slid up behind Rachel at the sink. Wrapping his arms around her, he kissed the back of her neck. She squirmed and shivered. He squeezed her tighter, growling into the nape of her neck.

A chubby fist gripped his pant leg and tugged. "Me, me, me," the voice below him squealed.

"You too?" Even after a year and a half, Morgan's heart hadn't ceased the feeling of being on the brink of bursting every time he looked at his baby girl.

He bent down and scooped Maddie Jo up, nuzzling her neck and blowing a raspberry while she screamed and giggled. Her twin brother, Brant, banged on the tray of his highchair with what could only be called a scowl etched across his forehead.

"Don't worry, buddy. I won't hurt her." Morgan chuckled and kissed Maddie Jo on the top of her head.

Little Brant had been the quieter of the twins from the day they were born. Neither had been fussy babies, but Brant had a quiet, serious demeanor from the very beginning. Rachel said he had an old soul. He looked more like a cranky old man if you asked Morgan.

A new song came over the radio, with the slide of a steel guitar and a good two-stepping rhythm. Morgan slid into the dining room, spinning in his socks on the hardwood floor with Maddie Jo in his arms. Rachel laughed and scooped up Brant from his highchair, joining them on the make-shift dancefloor. Brant's upturned little face shined with adoration as he looked up at his mama.

Maddie Jo rested her soft cheek against his chest as they

glided to the music, clutching Morgan's shirt in a tight fist. Heat radiated where she pressed herself against him, warming him through.

Light poured in through the tall windows and painted the polished wood in a golden hue. Rachel's long hair glistened in the sunlight as she spun Brant in a circle. Morgan danced in closer to her and shifted Maddie Jo so he could encompass all of them in his arms. He kissed the tops of both twins' heads before leaning in to plant a slower, lingering kiss on Rachel's smiling lips.

"I love you, Morgan Cross," Rachel whispered as all four of them swayed to the music.

Morgan had no doubt he made the right decision to stay here on the ranch and embrace the heritage passed down to him. He couldn't wait to fill their home with even more pattering feet and raise a family with this hard-working woman by his side. Together, they would pass down a legacy of strong women and honorable men to carry on the inheritance of faith and family that had been handed down for generations.

Continue reading about Morgan and Rachel's children in their own stories, beginning with Brant, Book 1 of the Cross Creek Ranch series.

〜

Did you enjoy Morgan and Rachel's story? I hope so! If you did, would you take a quick minute to leave a review? It can be as long or as short as you'd like—just a little something about why you liked the book.

Thanks for your support.

ALSO BY JODI BASYE

Cross Family Saga

Redeeming the Swindler

Redeeming the Prodigal

Redeeming the Outlaw

Redeeming the Shackled

Cross Creek Ranch

Morgan

Brant

Maddie Jo

Cash

Connect with me!
Instagram:
Jodi Basye (@jodibasyeauthor) • Instagram photos and videos

Facebook:
Jodi Basye - Author | Facebook

Goodreads:
Jodi Basye (Author of Redeeming the Prodigal) | Goodreads

Website:
www.jodibasye.com

Newsletter:
https://dl.bookfunnel.com/94611zqpab

Book club:
Jodi's Cowboys, Coffee & Clean Romance Online Book Club

Printed in Great Britain
by Amazon